aye: Yes, definitely.

me hearties: My loyal workers.

TE TALK

sea dogs: Experienced pirates.

lass: A young woman or girl.

plundering: Stealing.

arr: A favorite pirate expression used to show anger, sadness, or happiness.

GOOD PIRATE

Written by
Kari-Lynn Winters

pajamapress

Illustrated by
Dean Griffiths

First published in the United States and Canada in 2016

Text copyright © 2016 Kari-Lynn Winters
Illustration copyright © 2016 Dean Griffiths
This edition copyright © 2016 Pajama Press Inc.
This is a first edition.

10 9 8 7 6 5 4 3 2 1

 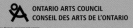

The publisher gratefully acknowledges the support of the Canada Council for the Arts and the Ontario Arts Council for its publishing program. We acknowledge the financial support of the Government of Canada through the Canada Book Fund (CBF) for our publishing activities.

Library and Archives Canada Cataloguing in Publication

Winters, Kari-Lynn, 1969-, author
      Good pirate / written by Kari-Lynn Winters ; illustrated
by Dean Griffiths.

ISBN 978-1-927485-80-4 (bound)

      I. Griffiths, Dean, 1967-, illustrator II. Title.

PS8645.I5745G65 2016   jC813'.6   C2015-906988-2

Publisher Cataloging-in-Publication Data (U.S.)

Names: Winters, Kari-Lynn, 1969-, author | Griffiths, Dean, 1967, illustrator
Title: Good pirate / written by Kari-Lynn Winters; illustrated by Dean Griffiths.
Description: Toronto, Ontario, Canada: Pajama Press, 2016. | Summary: "Augusta's pirate-captain father insists that pirates must be rotten, sneaky, and brainy. But Augusta prefers fanciness to foulness. Despite the crew's opposition, she sets out to prove that a successful pirate can be fancy, sneaky, and brainy, too" — Provided by publisher.
Identifiers: ISBN 978-1-92748-580-4 (hardcover)
Subjects: LCSH: Pirates – Juvenile fiction. | Dogs – Juvenile fiction. | Fathers and daughters – Juvenile fiction. | Values – Juvenile fiction.
Classification: LCC PZ7W568Go |DDC [E] – dc23

Edited by Ann Featherstone
Designed by Rebecca Bender

Manufactured by Qualibre Inc./Print Plus
Printed in China

Pajama Press Inc.
181 Carlaw Ave. Suite 207 Toronto, Ontario Canada, M4M 2S1

Distributed in Canada by UTP Distribution
5201 Dufferin Street Toronto, Ontario Canada, M3H 5T8

Distributed in the U.S. by Ingram Publisher Services
1 Ingram Blvd. La Vergne, TN 37086, USA

To me hearties, Marco and Jibber, who
have been my net and to the Land of
Lakes Senior Public School

–K.L.W.

To poop deck swabbing,
reekin', scurvy lass, Edna.

–D.G.

The foul captain, Barnacle Garrick,
and his sea pups practiced their plundering.

Them **Tuna Lubbers** stole me **booty** and I wants it back.

His daughter, the **fancy** Augusta, fixed her bandana and licked her fur clean.

But most important, me sea dogs, if yez be **BRAINY**, they won't trap ye.

Augusta couldn't stop herself...

Later, in the captain's cabin, Augusta secretly admired herself, wearing the last of the ship's booty.

Just then, Captain Garrick stomped over to Squid and Bones.

Shinin' yer boots? I've no use for a couple o' bucklin' fancies! Both of yez, into the brig!

Barnacle snarled at Scully.

Me crew has gotta know how to **raid**, not how to doll themselves up.

They be good and foul, captain, or they'll not be raidin'!

Augusta knew she needed to start being foul and useful, not fancy and useless.

Even though it felt wrong, for the next few days she kept the treasures in her pocket and practiced being **rotten, sneaky,** and **brainy**.

She smelled pure vanilla!

Augusta couldn't help herself. She licked the underside of her paws, opened the cap, and dabbed on the scent.

Just then...

In the brig, Squid and Bones whined and covered their noses.

Augusta ignored them, emptied her pockets, and devised a plan.

She untied the key, pushed it through
the grill, and undid the latch.

But something was wrong.

Augusta made
a new plan.

Captain Fishmonger gagged.

Somethin' reeks o' frillydog!

Meanwhile, Squid untied the captain
and his crew.

Shhh, it's all part of her sneaky
getaway plan.

She be **brainy**, even if she does gag
us with that fancy stench.

As she crossed the gangplank, Augusta broke her necklace and sent the pearls flying.

grill: A door's peephole, covered with a metal grid.

captain's cabin: A room on the ship that spans the width of the stern.

NAUTICAL TALK

captain: The boss of the ship.

gangplank: A board that can be used as a footbridge between two ships or a ship and a pier.